W9-BPK-206

I Love It When You Smile

Originally published in Great Britain as *It's Lovely When You Smile* by Puffin Books.

No part of this publication may be reproduced, stored in a retrieval system, or transmitted in any form
or by any means, electronic, mechanical, photocopying, recording, or otherwise, without written permission
of the publisher. For information regarding permission, write to HarperCollins Children's Books, a division of
HarperCollins Publishers, 1350 Avenue of the Americas, New York, NY 10019.

ISBN-13: 978-0-545-16505-1
ISBN-10: 0-545-16505-9

Text copyright © 2005 by Sam McBratney. Illustrations copyright © 2005 by Charles Fuge. All rights reserved.
Published by Scholastic Inc., 557 Broadway, New York, NY 10012, by arrangement with HarperCollins
Children's Books, a division of HarperCollins Publishers. SCHOLASTIC and associated logos
are trademarks and/or registered trademarks of Scholastic Inc.

12 11 10 9 8 7 6 5 4 3 2   9 10 11 12 13 14/0

Printed in the U.S.A.   40

First Scholastic printing, April 2009

I Love It When You Smile

Sam McBratney
Charles Fuge

SCHOLASTIC INC.
New York Toronto London Auckland Sydney
Mexico City New Delhi Hong Kong Buenos Aires

It was a lovely summer morning,
but Roo was feeling grumpy
and he didn't know why.

He was feeling so grumpy that
he didn't even want to play.

"What's wrong with you this morning?"
asked his mother.
"Nothing," said Roo.
"You should smile," his mother said.
"Everybody feels better
when they smile."

But Little Roo **wasn't** in a smiling mood today,
not even when his mother **tickled** him gently.
"Did I see a tiny **smile?**" she asked.
"Just one?"

"**No!**" said Roo.
"**You didn't.**"

It was the
kind of game that
little kangaroos
love to play!

His mom reached out
and flipped
him up
head over heels.

But would it work this grumpy morning?

No. Little Roo did **not** smile.

Not even a teeny-weeny bit.

His mother skipped into a hollow

tree where they liked to play.

She popped her head through

a hole in the trunk.

"Smile!"

"I still don't want to," said Little Roo.

"Oh dear," said his mom. So she gathered up some dry leaves, tossed them into the air, and all the leaves came down on Little Roo.

He looked **so** funny!
"I think I can see a **smile** this time,"
his mom said, and **laughed.**
"Just a little
one . . . ?"

"You don't," said Roo. "I'm NOT smiling."

"Oh well," his mother said with a sigh.

It was time for breakfast.

Little Roo's mom lifted him up. "Let's go down
the hill together and find something to eat."

"I'm not hungry," said Roo grumpily.

"But I'm hungry," said his mom.

"Come on."

"Hold on tight!"

And off they went.

Halfway down the hill there was a hole.

It wasn't a deep hole, but it was a wide hole,

and a **muddy-at-the-bottom** hole.

"Look out!" cried Roo.

But his mom was doing silly hops

from side to side instead

of looking

where

she

was

going

AND . . .

...slippity

...slippity

...slide

and...

...slop!
Right into
the hole.

What a mess.
WHAT A
MESS!

Roo himself was **muddy all over**.
Then he looked at his mother, who was soaking wet and
slimy from the **tops of her ears** to the **tips of her toes**.

And Little Roo couldn't do anything else.

He just
had
to . . .

... smile!

"I love it when you smile."